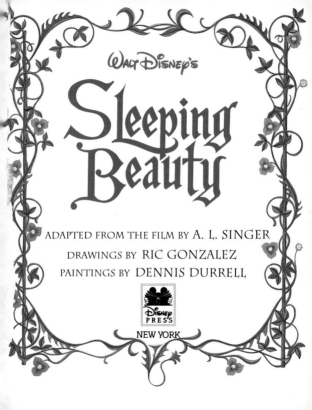

Walt Disney's
Sleeping Beauty

ADAPTED FROM THE FILM BY A. L. SINGER

DRAWINGS BY RIC GONZALEZ

PAINTINGS BY DENNIS DURRELL

Disney PRESS

NEW YORK

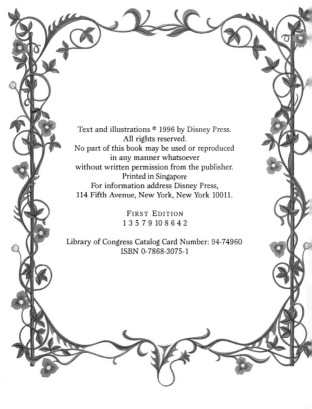

Printed in Singapore
For information address Disney Press,
114 Fifth Avenue, New York, New York 10011.

FIRST EDITION
1 3 5 7 9 10 8 6 4 2

Library of Congress Catalog Card Number: 94-74960
ISBN 0-7868-3075-1

Walt Disney's

Sleeping Beauty

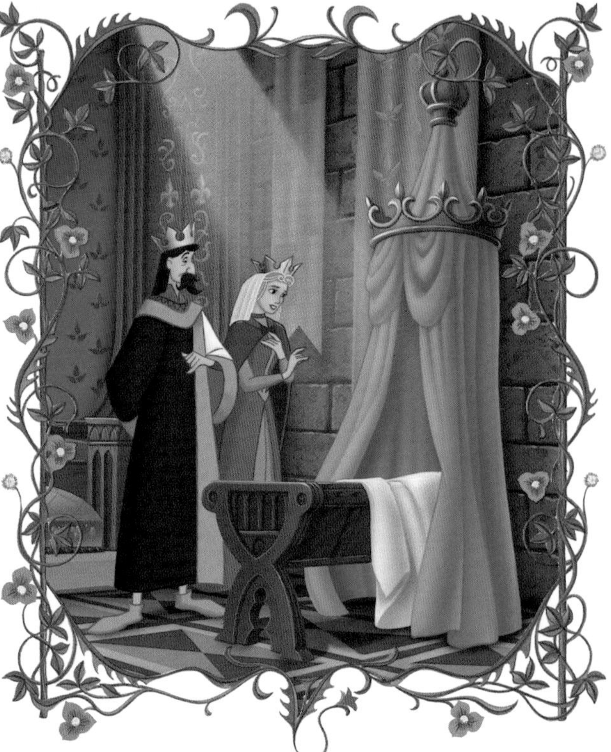

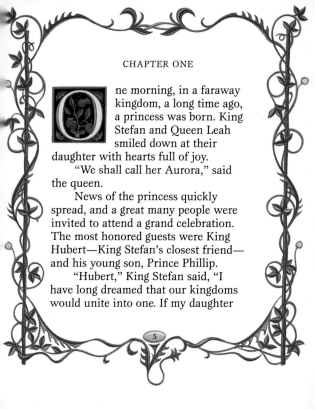

ne morning, in a faraway kingdom, a long time ago, a princess was born. King Stefan and Queen Leah smiled down at their daughter with hearts full of joy.

"We shall call her Aurora," said the queen.

News of the princess quickly spread, and a great many people were invited to attend a grand celebration. The most honored guests were King Hubert—King Stefan's closest friend—and his young son, Prince Phillip.

"Hubert," King Stefan said, "I have long dreamed that our kingdoms would unite into one. If my daughter

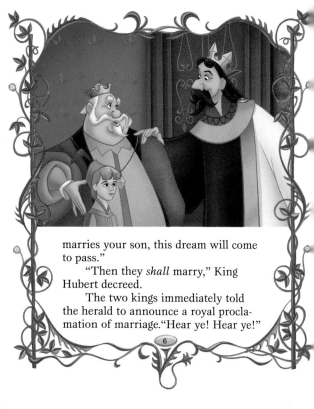

marries your son, this dream will come
to pass."

"Then they *shall* marry," King
Hubert decreed.

The two kings immediately told
the herald to announce a royal procla-
mation of marriage. "Hear ye! Hear ye!"

the herald shouted. "Their Majesties King Stefan and King Hubert hereby announce the betrothal of Princess Aurora to Prince Phillip!"

The herald made another declaration: "Announcing their most honored and exalted excellencies, the three good fairies: Flora, Fauna, and Merryweather!"

A beam of light shimmered down through the window. In that light were three winged fairies. Each had a magic wand and was dressed in a brightly colored gown.

"Your Majesties," Flora announced, "each of us the child may bless, with a single gift—no more, no less."

Flora stepped to the cradle, waved her magic wand in a circle, and said, "Little Princess, my gift shall be the gift of beauty."

Then Fauna stepped forward, waved her magic wand, and said, "Tiny Princess, my gift shall be the gift of song."

At last it was Merryweather's turn. She went to the cradle with her

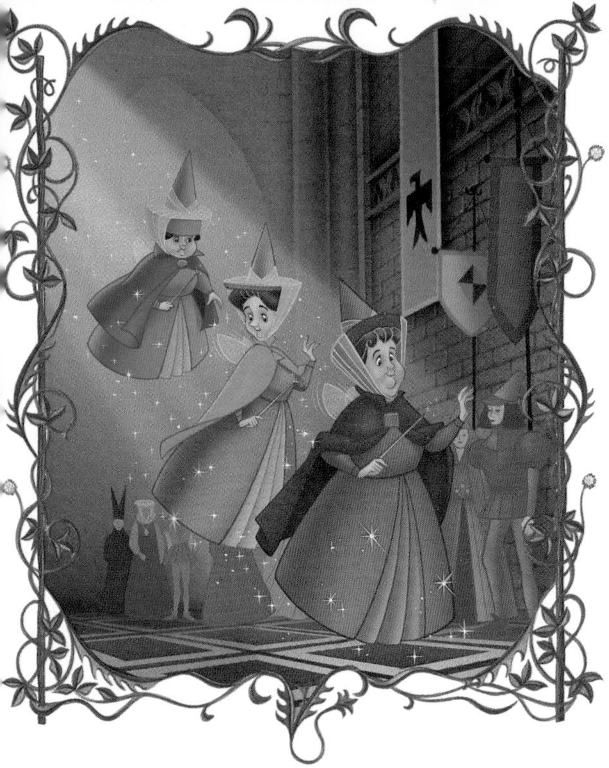

wand and said, "Sweet Princess, my gift shall be the—"

BOOOOM! With a sudden *crack* of thunder, the room grew dark. Then a bolt of lightning struck the center of the room. Hissing green flames shot upward from the floor, and a dark figure appeared—the figure of a tall woman shrouded in black. She held a long, thin staff with a glowing knob on top. An ugly black raven perched on the knob.

"It's Maleficent!" Fauna whispered. "What does she want here?"

"Shhhhh!" Flora warned.

Maleficent's voice was smooth and low, but it was filled with coldness. "I really felt quite distressed at not receiving an invitation," said Maleficent.

"You weren't wanted!" blurted

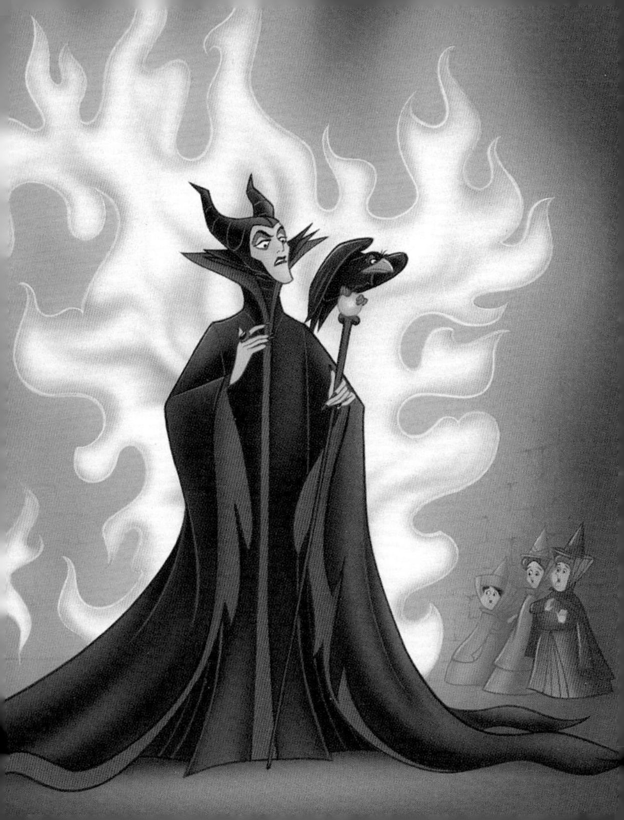

Merryweather.

Maleficent began to pet her raven gently. "Oh dear, I had hoped it was due to some oversight. Well, in that event, I'd best be on my way."

With that, she turned to leave.

Queen Leah spoke up. "And you're not offended, Your Excellency?"

"Why, no, Your Majesty," Maleficent said. "And to show I bear no ill will, I, too, shall bestow a gift on the child."

Maleficent's face grew dark with hate. "Listen well, all of you!" she bellowed. "Before the sun sets on her sixteenth birthday, the princess shall prick her finger on the spindle of a spinning wheel and *die*!" As she spoke, the small knob on top of her staff grew into a crystal ball, aglow

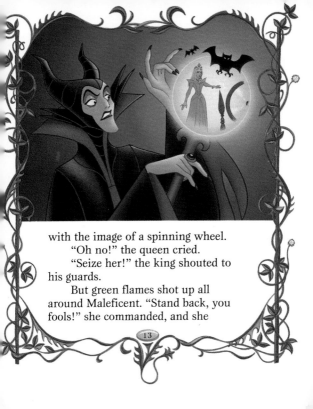

with the image of a spinning wheel.

"Oh no!" the queen cried.

"Seize her!" the king shouted to his guards.

But green flames shot up all around Maleficent. "Stand back, you fools!" she commanded, and she

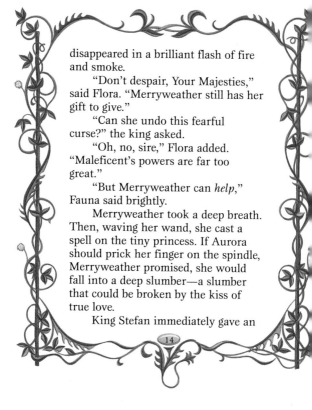

disappeared in a brilliant flash of fire and smoke.

"Don't despair, Your Majesties," said Flora. "Merryweather still has her gift to give."

"Can she undo this fearful curse?" the king asked.

"Oh, no, sire," Flora added. "Maleficent's powers are far too great."

"But Merryweather can *help*," Fauna said brightly.

Merryweather took a deep breath. Then, waving her wand, she cast a spell on the tiny princess. If Aurora should prick her finger on the spindle, Merryweather promised, she would fall into a deep slumber—a slumber that could be broken by the kiss of true love.

King Stefan immediately gave an

order for all the spinning wheels in the kingdom to be burned.

A fire soon blazed in the royal courtyard, fueled by spinning wheels new and old. Something else had to be done to protect Aurora—but what?

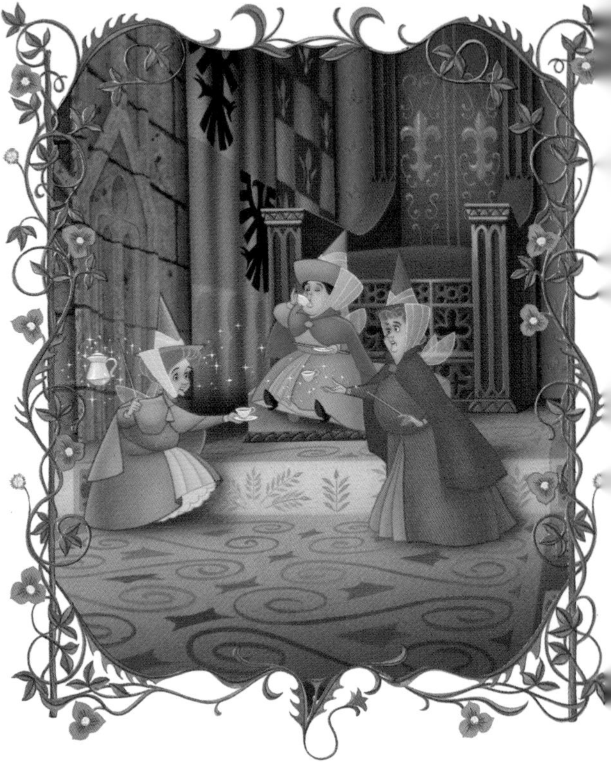

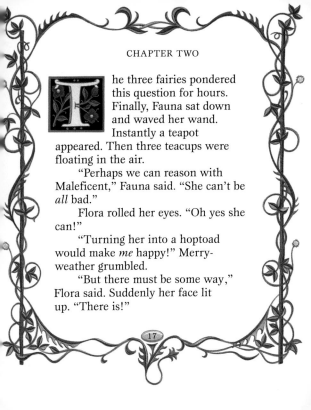

CHAPTER TWO

The three fairies pondered this question for hours. Finally, Fauna sat down and waved her wand.

Instantly a teapot appeared. Then three teacups were floating in the air.

"Perhaps we can reason with Maleficent," Fauna said. "She can't be *all* bad."

Flora rolled her eyes. "Oh yes she can!"

"Turning her into a hoptoad would make *me* happy!" Merryweather grumbled.

"But there must be some way," Flora said. Suddenly her face lit up. "There is!"

"What is it, Flora?" Fauna asked.

"Follow me!" Fauna said.

Zzzing! With a sweep of her wand, she made herself shrink to the size of a butterfly.

Zzzing! Zzzing! Flora and Merryweather did the same. Then they hid themselves inside a small decorative box on a table near the throne.

Now no one would hear them.

"We must do something Maleficent won't be expecting," said Flora.

"But she knows *everything*," Merryweather said.

"Maleficent doesn't know anything about love or kindness or the joy of helping others," said Fauna.

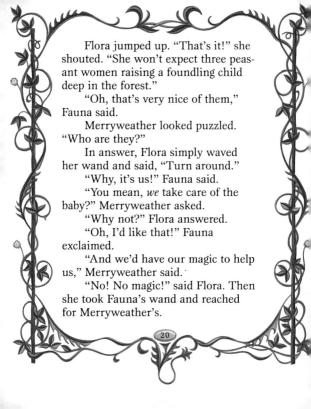

Flora jumped up. "That's it!" she shouted. "She won't expect three peasant women raising a foundling child deep in the forest."

"Oh, that's very nice of them," Fauna said.

Merryweather looked puzzled. "Who are they?"

In answer, Flora simply waved her wand and said, "Turn around."

"Why, it's us!" Fauna said.

"You mean, *we* take care of the baby?" Merryweather asked.

"Why not?" Flora answered.

"Oh, I'd like that!" Fauna exclaimed.

"And we'd have our magic to help us," Merryweather said.

"No! No magic!" said Flora. Then she took Fauna's wand and reached for Merryweather's.

20

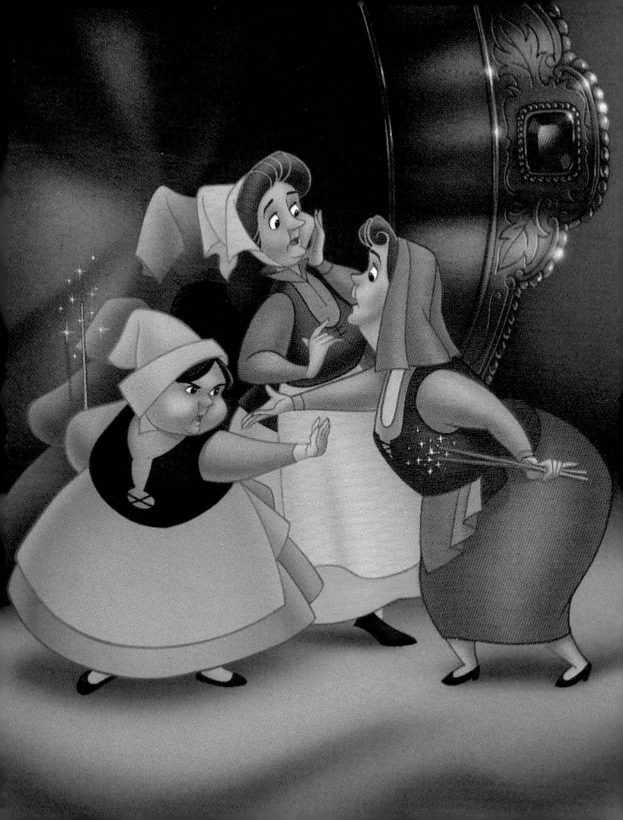

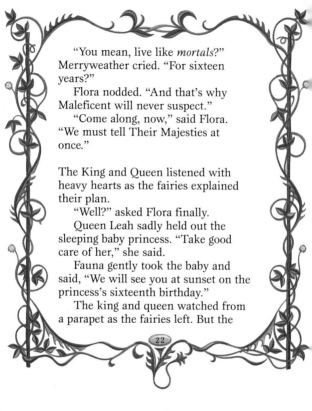

"You mean, live like *mortals*?" Merryweather cried. "For sixteen years?"

Flora nodded. "And that's why Maleficent will never suspect."

"Come along, now," said Flora. "We must tell Their Majesties at once."

The King and Queen listened with heavy hearts as the fairies explained their plan.

"Well?" asked Flora finally.

Queen Leah sadly held out the sleeping baby princess. "Take good care of her," she said.

Fauna gently took the baby and said, "We will see you at sunset on the princess's sixteenth birthday."

The king and queen watched from a parapet as the fairies left. But the

fairies made sure not to look back,
because the grief on Their Majesties'
faces would have been enough to melt
a heart of stone.

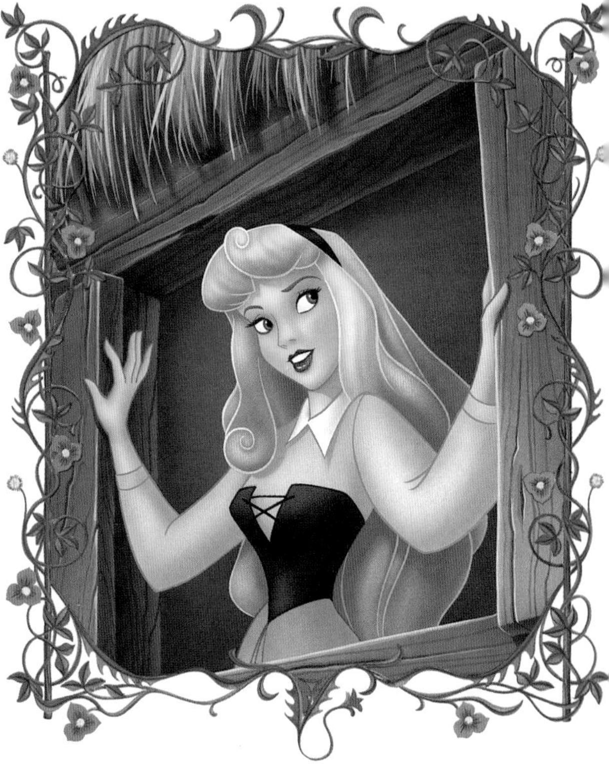

he years passed quickly as the fairies cared for the princess. In their humble cottage deep in the woods Aurora became more and more beautiful as each day passed. Her hair was golden, and her eyes sparkled like diamonds. But it was because of her deep red lips that the fairies named her Briar Rose. Aurora knew herself only by that name—her true identity remained a secret.

For King Stefan and Queen Leah, the time passed slowly. The entire kingdom fell into gloom over the missing princess. For sixteen years thunder boomed and lightning flashed all around Maleficent's decaying castle in the Forbidden Mountains. On the eve

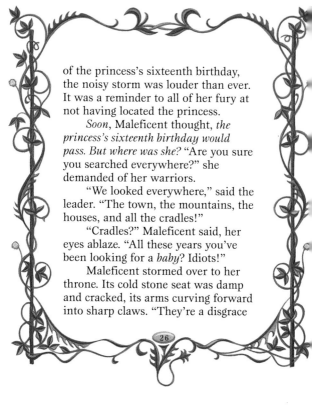

of the princess's sixteenth birthday, the noisy storm was louder than ever. It was a reminder to all of her fury at not having located the princess.

Soon, Maleficent thought, *the princess's sixteenth birthday would pass. But where was she?* "Are you sure you searched everywhere?" she demanded of her warriors.

"We looked everywhere," said the leader. "The town, the mountains, the houses, and all the cradles!"

"Cradles?" Maleficent said, her eyes ablaze. "All these years you've been looking for a *baby*? Idiots!"

Maleficent stormed over to her throne. Its cold stone seat was damp and cracked, its arms curving forward into sharp claws. "They're a disgrace

26

to the forces of evil," she said to her
raven.

"You are my last chance, my pet,"
she said to the bird. "Search for a
maid of sixteen with hair of gold and
lips red as the rose. Go!"

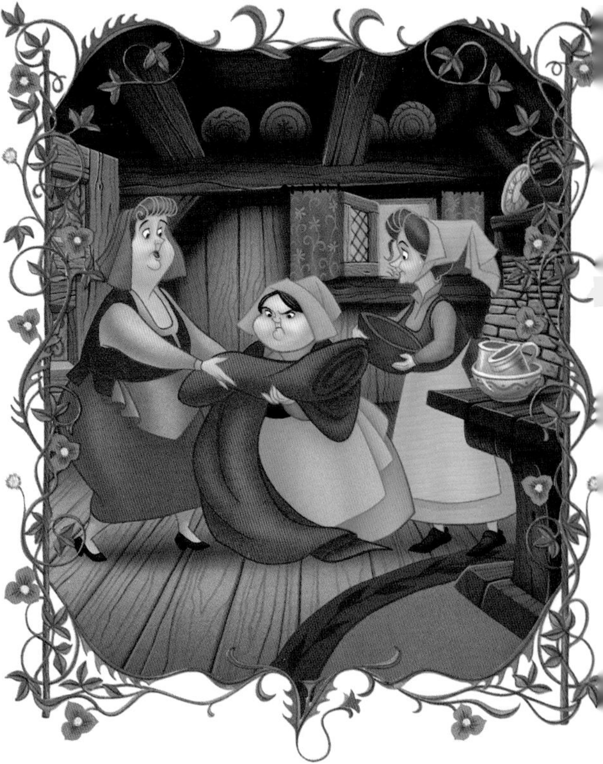

CHAPTER FOUR

T he morning sky promised a beautiful day for Briar Rose's birthday. By day's end, the spell would be broken, and the fairies would be taking Briar Rose home. But before they did, they planned to give her a wonderful surprise party.

First they sent Briar Rose outside to pick some berries. Then they set to work.

"Imagine! A real birthday party!" Merryweather squealed.

"With a real birthday cake!" Fauna added.

"And a dress a princess can be proud of!" Flora beamed.

"I'll bake the cake," said Fauna.

"And I'll make the dress," Flora

29

said, clapping her hands together.

"But you can't sew, and Fauna has never baked," Merryweather said. "I think we should use magic."

"Oh, all you have to do is follow the book," Fauna replied.

Flora pulled up a stool next to Merryweather. "Up here, dear. You can be the dummy."

At the kitchen table, Fauna stirred a big glop of lumpy batter as she consulted a cookbook.

Flora sighed as she marked off Briar Rose's height on the fabric. "Gracious, how that child has grown!"

Merryweather nodded sadly. "It seems only yesterday that we brought her here."

Fauna sighed fondly. "Just a tiny baby."

"After today she'll be a princess," Merryweather sniffled, "and we won't

have any Briar Rose."

"We all knew this day had to come," said Flora.

"But why did it have to come so soon?" Fauna asked tearfully.

Not far away, Briar Rose sang as she stepped lightly through the woods,

an empty wicker basket on her arm. So lovely was her voice that even the birds stopped to hear her. Before long she had her own private audience.

Clear across the forest, someone else was enchanted by Briar Rose's song—a handsome young man dressed in the finest silk clothing.

"Samson!" he called to his horse.

"Do you hear that? Let's find out who that is!"

Samson raced off, until—*BONK!* The horse stopped short. Above him was a large tree branch. Samson turned around to look for his master, but there was no one in the saddle anymore.

The young man was sitting in a

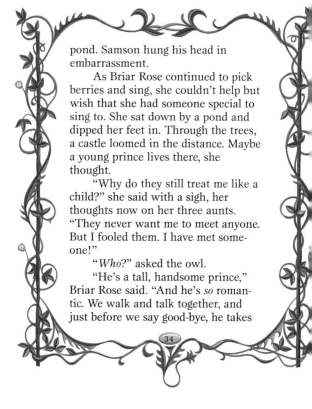

pond. Samson hung his head in embarrassment.

As Briar Rose continued to pick berries and sing, she couldn't help but wish that she had someone special to sing to. She sat down by a pond and dipped her feet in. Through the trees, a castle loomed in the distance. Maybe a young prince lives there, she thought.

"Why do they still treat me like a child?" she said with a sigh, her thoughts now on her three aunts. "They never want me to meet anyone. But I fooled them. I have met someone!"

"*Who*?" asked the owl.

"He's a tall, handsome prince," Briar Rose said. "And he's *so* romantic. We walk and talk together, and just before we say good-bye, he takes

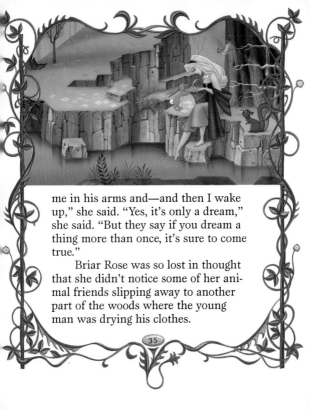

me in his arms and—and then I wake up," she said. "Yes, it's only a dream," she said. "But they say if you dream a thing more than once, it's sure to come true."

Briar Rose was so lost in thought that she didn't notice some of her animal friends slipping away to another part of the woods where the young man was drying his clothes.

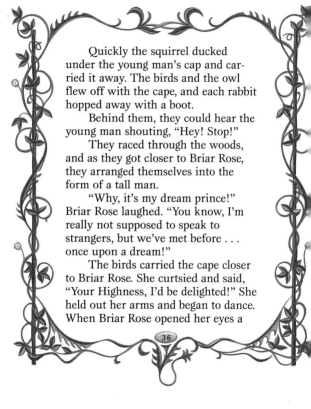

Quickly the squirrel ducked under the young man's cap and carried it away. The birds and the owl flew off with the cape, and each rabbit hopped away with a boot.

Behind them, they could hear the young man shouting, "Hey! Stop!"

They raced through the woods, and as they got closer to Briar Rose, they arranged themselves into the form of a tall man.

"Why, it's my dream prince!" Briar Rose laughed. "You know, I'm really not supposed to speak to strangers, but we've met before . . . once upon a dream!"

The birds carried the cape closer to Briar Rose. She curtsied and said, "Your Highness, I'd be delighted!" She held out her arms and began to dance. When Briar Rose opened her eyes a

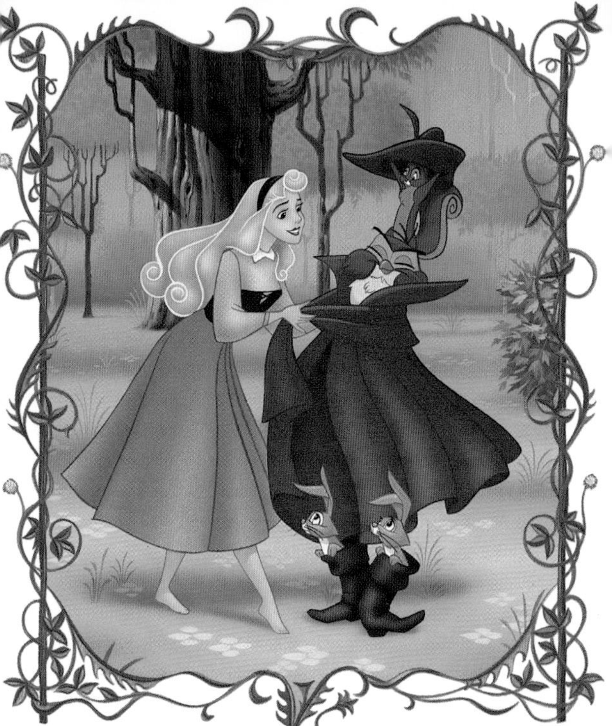

few moments later, she looked right
into the face of—a very real young
man!

"I didn't mean to frighten you,"
the young man said.

"It's just that you're a . . . a . . .
stranger," she replied.

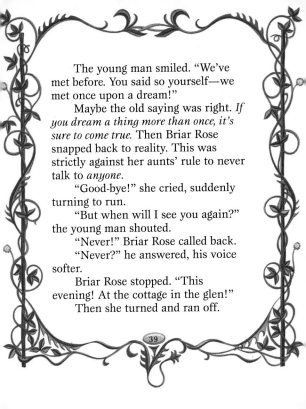

The young man smiled. "We've met before. You said so yourself—we met once upon a dream!"

Maybe the old saying was right. *If you dream a thing more than once, it's sure to come true.* Then Briar Rose snapped back to reality. This was strictly against her aunts' rule to never talk to *anyone.*

"Good-bye!" she cried, suddenly turning to run.

"But when will I see you again?" the young man shouted.

"Never!" Briar Rose called back.

"Never?" he answered, his voice softer.

Briar Rose stopped. "This evening! At the cottage in the glen!"

Then she turned and ran off.

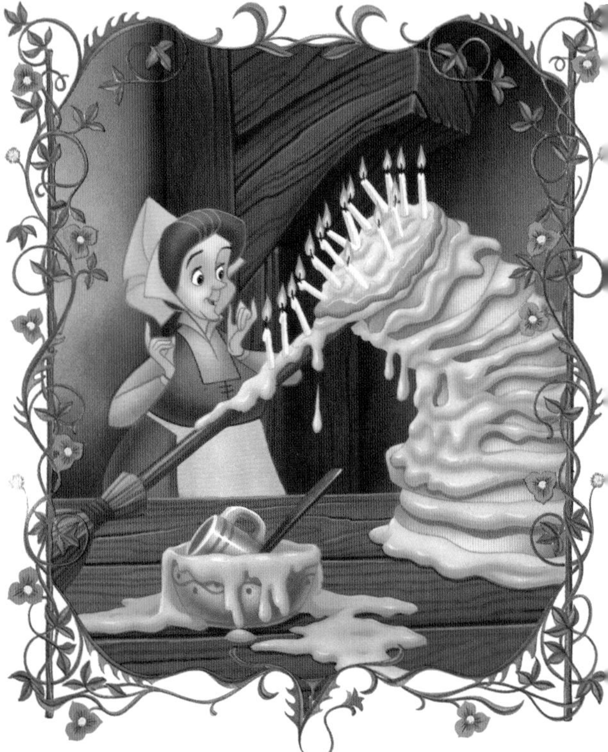

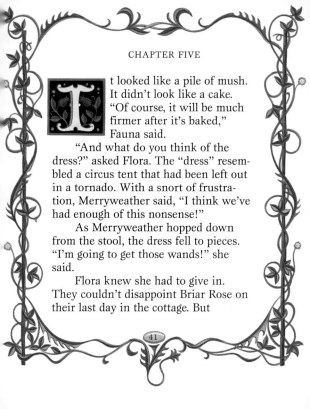

t looked like a pile of mush. It didn't look like a cake. "Of course, it will be much firmer after it's baked," Fauna said.

"And what do you think of the dress?" asked Flora. The "dress" resembled a circus tent that had been left out in a tornado. With a snort of frustration, Merryweather said, "I think we've had enough of this nonsense!"

As Merryweather hopped down from the stool, the dress fell to pieces. "I'm going to get those wands!" she said.

Flora knew she had to give in. They couldn't disappoint Briar Rose on their last day in the cottage. But

using the wands could be dangerous.
They gave off a powerful light that
twinkled with magic dust that
Maleficent's spies might notice.

"All right," Flora said. "Close the
windows and plug up every cranny!"
They made sure even the tiniest knot-
hole in the cottage was plugged. Then,
with a grand wave, they began to pre-
pare for the party.

Zzzing! Merryweather made the bucket, mop, and broom burst to life. They bustled about, cleaning the cottage.

Zzzing! Fauna created a magnificent cake out of the ingredients on the table.

Zzzing! Flora made the material come together to form a stunning pink gown.

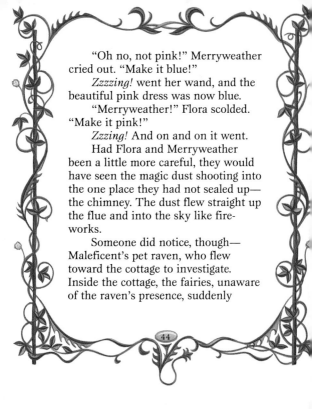

"Oh no, not pink!" Merryweather cried out. "Make it blue!"

Zzzing! went her wand, and the beautiful pink dress was now blue.

"Merryweather!" Flora scolded. "Make it pink!"

Zzing! And on and on it went.

Had Flora and Merryweather been a little more careful, they would have seen the magic dust shooting into the one place they had not sealed up— the chimney. The dust flew straight up the flue and into the sky like fireworks.

Someone did notice, though— Maleficent's pet raven, who flew toward the cottage to investigate. Inside the cottage, the fairies, unaware of the raven's presence, suddenly

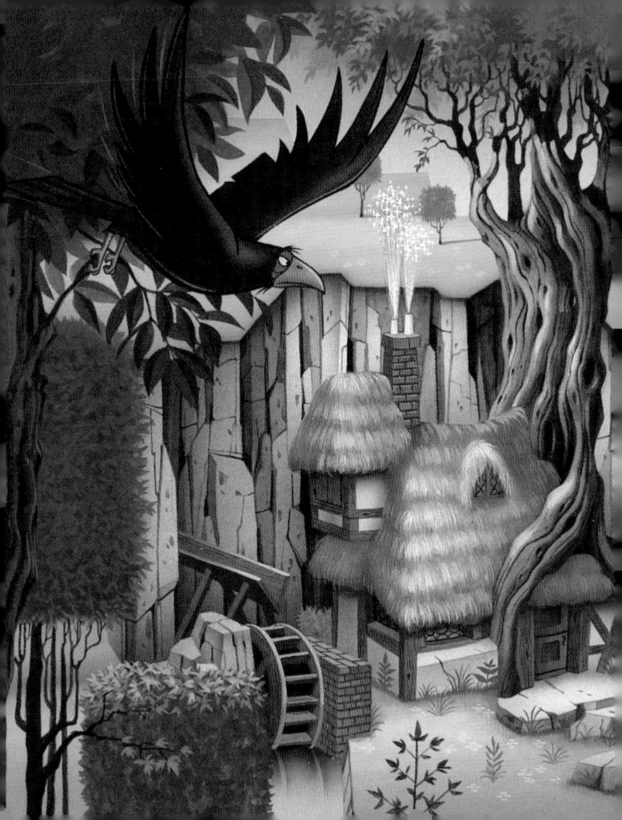

heard Briar Rose's sweet singing in
the distance.

"Rose is back!" Flora exclaimed.

Fauna lit the candles on the cake,
and Merryweather waved her wand
one last time. *Zzzing!* The dress turned
blue. Then they ran to hide on the
stairs.

"Aunt Flora!" came Briar Rose's
voice from outside.

"Where is everybody?" Briar Rose
asked as she entered the cottage.

"Surprise!" the fairies yelled.
"Happy birthday!"

"This is the happiest day of my
life," Briar Rose shouted. "Oh, just
wait till you meet him!"

"Him?" Fauna repeated

"You've met a stranger?" Flora
asked.

Briar Rose smiled. "Oh, he's not a

stranger. We've met before. Once upon
a dream."

"She's in love," Fauna said.

"This is terrible!" Flora cried.

"Why?" Briar Rose asked. "After
all, I am sixteen."

"Rose, you're already betrothed,"
said Fauna.

"Since the day you were born,"

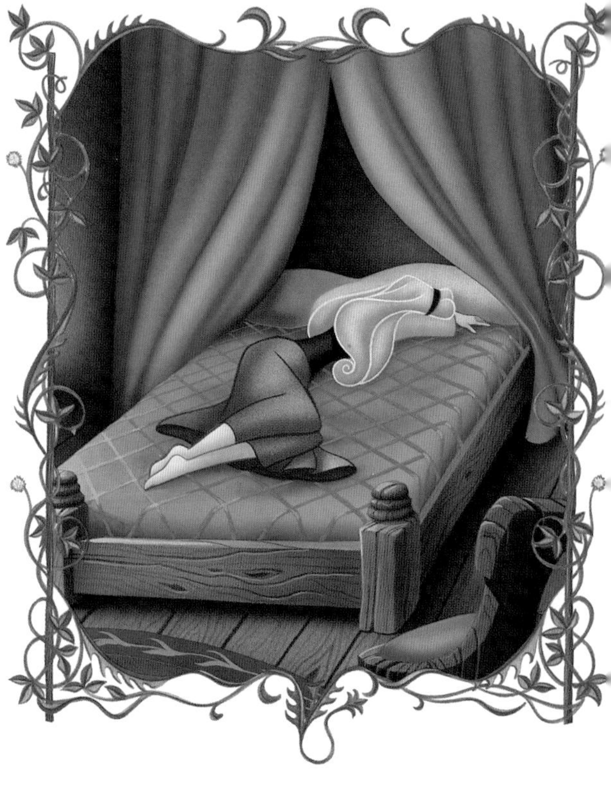

Merryweather said, nodding.

"To Prince Phillip," Fauna added.

"Your name is Princess Aurora," said Fauna. "Tonight we're taking you back to your parents, King Stefan and Queen Leah."

"But he's coming here tonight. I promised to meet him!"

"You must never see that young man again," said Flora.

"No," cried Briar Rose. "No! I can't believe it!" Her voice was choking with grief. She put her hands to her face and ran upstairs.

Merryweather sighed. "And we thought she'd be so happy . . . ," she murmured. She looked out at the forest and watched as a large bird flew away from the cottage. It never occurred to her that it was Maleficent's raven.

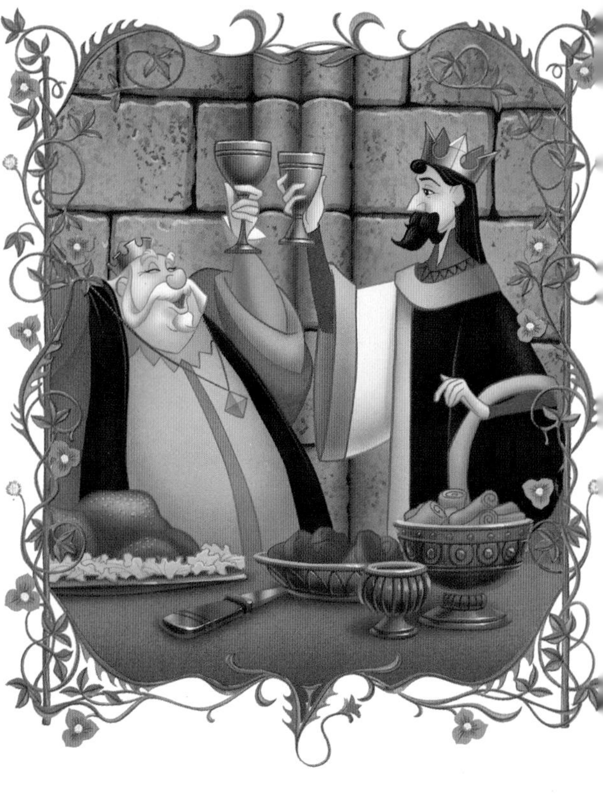

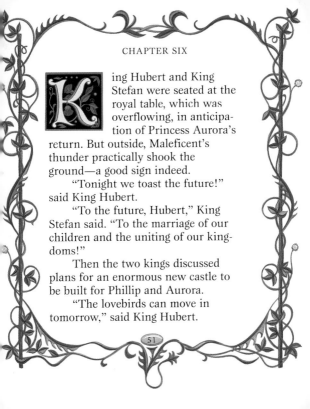

CHAPTER SIX

King Hubert and King Stefan were seated at the royal table, which was overflowing, in anticipation of Princess Aurora's return. But outside, Maleficent's thunder practically shook the ground—a good sign indeed.

"Tonight we toast the future!" said King Hubert.

"To the future, Hubert," King Stefan said. "To the marriage of our children and the uniting of our kingdoms!"

Then the two kings discussed plans for an enormous new castle to be built for Phillip and Aurora.

"The lovebirds can move in tomorrow," said King Hubert.

"Tomorrow?" King Stefan said. "But Hubert, they're not even married."

"We'll take care of that tonight!" King Hubert said.

"But Aurora knows nothing about this," said King Stefan. "It may come as a shock to her."

"My Phillip a shock? What's wrong with *my* Phillip?"

"Nothing," King Stefan protested.

Then the two kings began to argue. "Now see here, you blustering old windbag!" shouted King Stefan.

"Windbag?" King Hubert's face was red with anger. He reached out to grab a weapon—anything. The first thing his fingers clenched was a cooked fish. "On guard, sir!"

Grabbing a platter like a shield, King Stefan said, "This means war!"

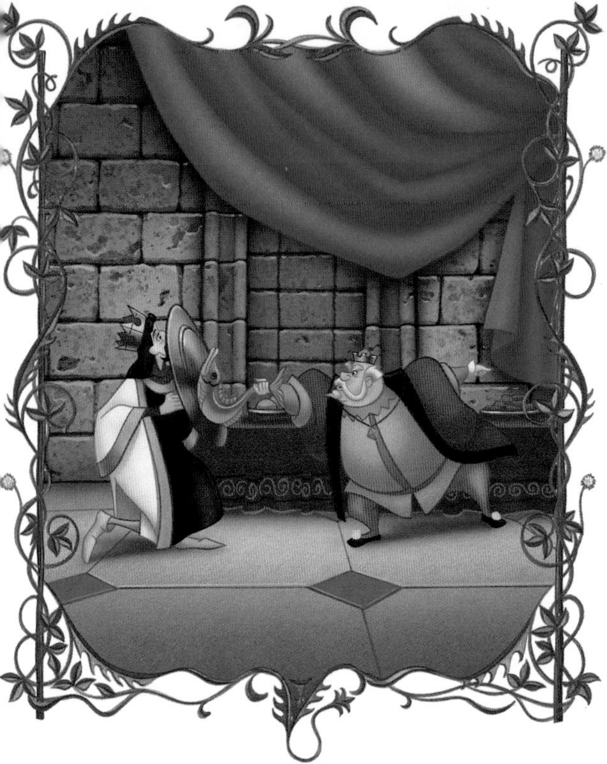

He raised the fish high and brought it down over King Stefan's head.

Splaaaaatt! The fish squashed against King Stefan's platter.

The two kings stopped, and in an instant they both began to laugh. "Our children are bound to fall in love with each other," King Hubert said.

As they picked up their glasses for another toast, a herald cried, "Prince Phillip!"

King Hubert bolted out of the dining room and ran into the courtyard. "Phillip!" King Hubert shouted. "You can't meet your bride looking like that!"

"But I *have* met her, Father!" Prince Phillip said.

"Where?" King Hubert asked.

"Once upon a dream!" Phillip

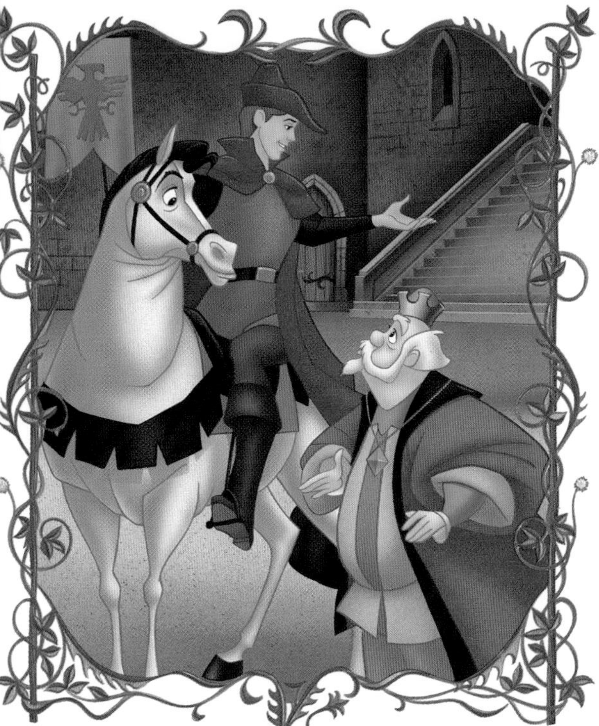

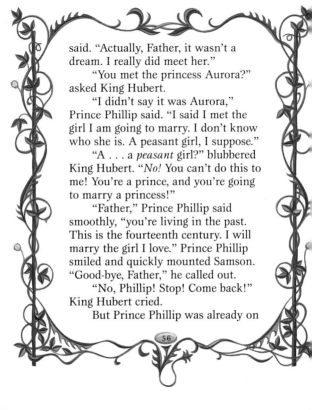

said. "Actually, Father, it wasn't a dream. I really did meet her."

"You met the princess Aurora?" asked King Hubert.

"I didn't say it was Aurora," Prince Phillip said. "I said I met the girl I am going to marry. I don't know who she is. A peasant girl, I suppose."

"A . . . a *peasant* girl?" blubbered King Hubert. "*No!* You can't do this to me! You're a prince, and you're going to marry a princess!"

"Father," Prince Phillip said smoothly, "you're living in the past. This is the fourteenth century. I will marry the girl I love." Prince Phillip smiled and quickly mounted Samson. "Good-bye, Father," he called out.

"No, Phillip! Stop! Come back!" King Hubert cried.

But Prince Phillip was already on

his way. He wasn't going to have his marriage arranged for him. He knew that Princess Aurora couldn't be lovelier and sweeter than the girl he'd met today.

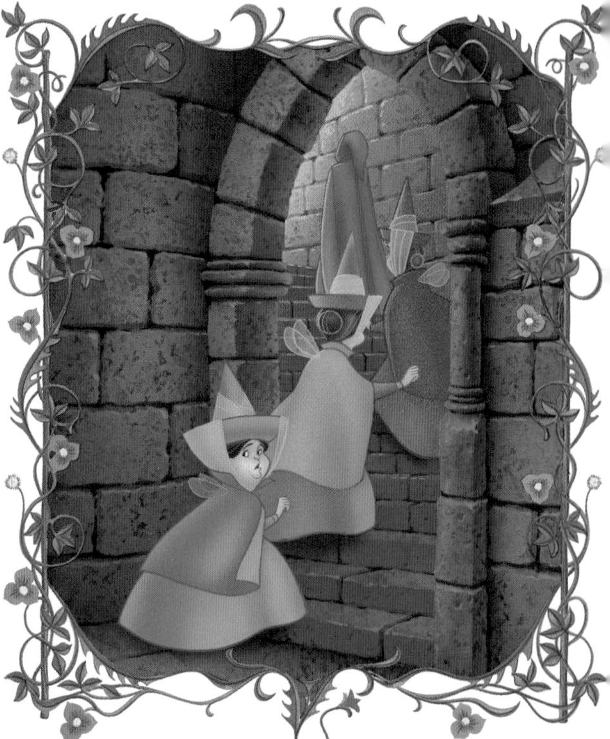

urora shivered as she crossed the bridge to the castle. The fairies wanted no one to see or hear them. It was hard for Princess Aurora to think of herself as anything but Briar Rose. After so many years in the modest little cottage, Aurora could scarcely believe that this was her real home.

She kept thinking about the young man she'd met in the forest. Right about now, he'd be arriving at the cottage to meet her, but she would never see him again.

They walked up a winding set of stairs to a small, dark room. "Bolt the door and pull the drapes," said Flora.

Flora gently led Aurora to a seat

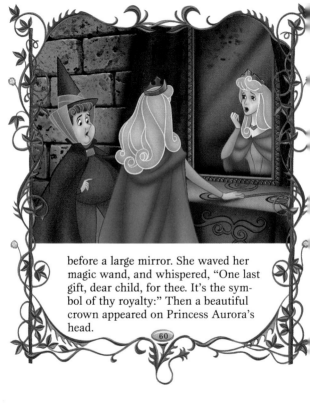

before a large mirror. She waved her
magic wand, and whispered, "One last
gift, dear child, for thee. It's the sym-
bol of thy royalty." Then a beautiful
crown appeared on Princess Aurora's
head.

The fairies sighed happily as Aurora turned to face the mirror.

The girl in the reflection was a stranger—a princess, not Briar Rose. With an anguished sob, she buried her face in her arms and wept.

"Let her have a few moments alone," Flora said.

Quietly they left the room. "It's that boy she met," Merryweather whispered.

"Whatever are we going to do?" Fauna asked.

Suddenly the fireplace inside Aurora's room grew dark and a small green ball of glowing light appeared. Aurora rose from her seat and slowly walked toward the fireplace.

A dark image appeared around the light. Aurora did not recognize the

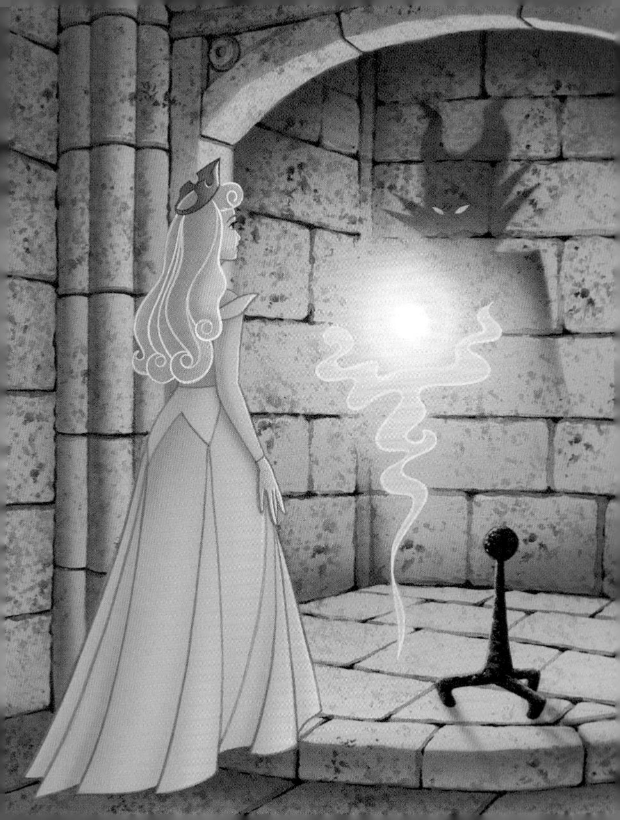

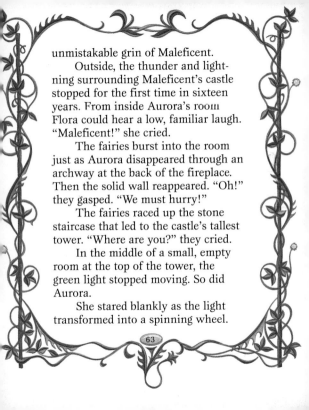

unmistakable grin of Maleficent.

Outside, the thunder and lightning surrounding Maleficent's castle stopped for the first time in sixteen years. From inside Aurora's room Flora could hear a low, familiar laugh. "Maleficent!" she cried.

The fairies burst into the room just as Aurora disappeared through an archway at the back of the fireplace. Then the solid wall reappeared. "Oh!" they gasped. "We must hurry!"

The fairies raced up the stone staircase that led to the castle's tallest tower. "Where are you?" they cried.

In the middle of a small, empty room at the top of the tower, the green light stopped moving. So did Aurora.

She stared blankly as the light transformed into a spinning wheel.

On it, a long spindle glistened with unearthly light.

Slowly she reached her finger toward it.

"Rose! *Don't touch anything!*" the

fairies cried all at once.

"Touch the spindle!" Maleficent
hissed, invisible in the darkened room.

Aurora's eyes glazed over. Once
again, she reached toward the blinding

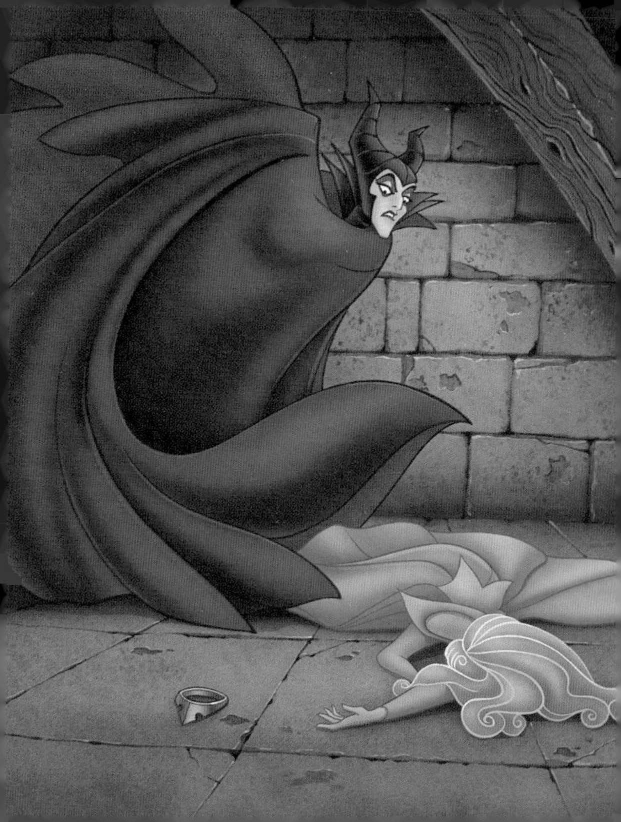

white pinpoint of light.

Then the fairies barged in.

As the door crashed open, they gasped. There in a cloud of smoke stood Maleficent. "You thought you could defeat me—*me*, the mistress of all evil!" shouted Maleficent. "Well, here's your precious princess!" she said.

In the smoky swirl, Aurora lay motionless on the floor, her eyes closed.

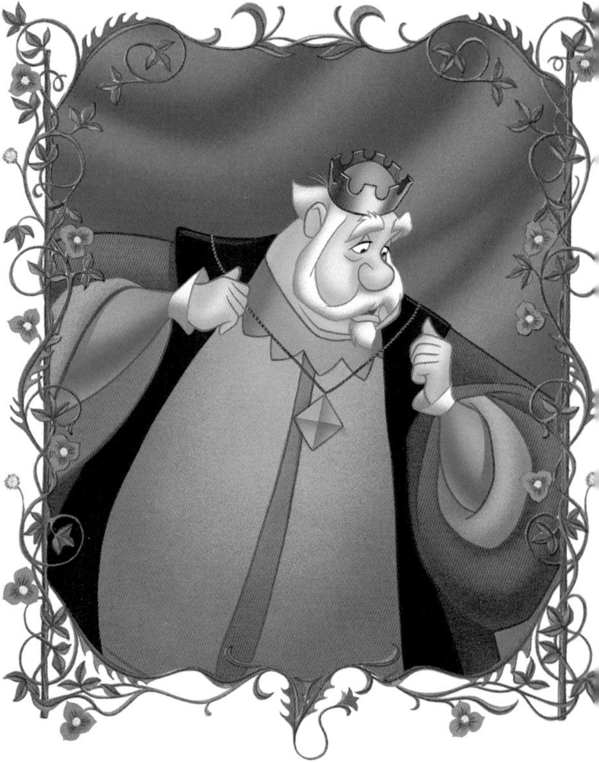

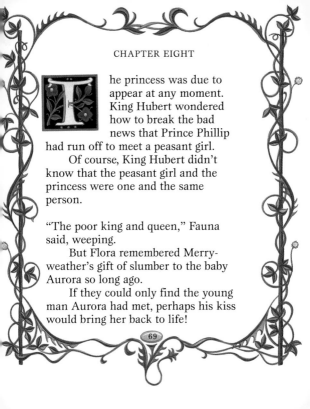

he princess was due to appear at any moment. King Hubert wondered how to break the bad news that Prince Phillip had run off to meet a peasant girl.

Of course, King Hubert didn't know that the peasant girl and the princess were one and the same person.

"The poor king and queen," Fauna said, weeping.

But Flora remembered Merryweather's gift of slumber to the baby Aurora so long ago.

If they could only find the young man Aurora had met, perhaps his kiss would bring her back to life!

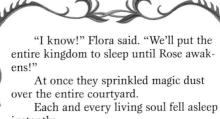

"I know!" Flora said. "We'll put the entire kingdom to sleep until Rose awakens!"

At once they sprinkled magic dust over the entire courtyard.

Each and every living soul fell asleep instantly.

When Flora reached the throne room she heard King Hubert say, "You see, Stefan, Phillip seems to have fallen in love with some peasant girl." Then he yawned.

"Where did he meet her?" Flora asked King Hubert excitedly.

"He met her once upon a dream," he answered.

Those were the same words Aurora had used after she met the young man in the woods! Flora remembered. Could he have been Prince Phillip? she wondered.

If the prince's love for Aurora was as

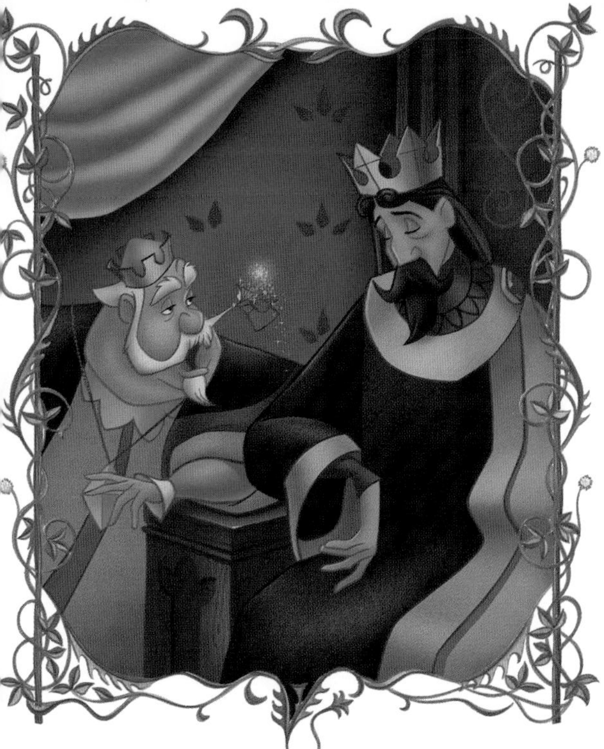

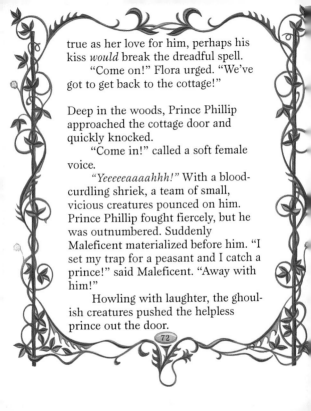

true as her love for him, perhaps his kiss *would* break the dreadful spell.

"Come on!" Flora urged. "We've got to get back to the cottage!"

Deep in the woods, Prince Phillip approached the cottage door and quickly knocked.

"Come in!" called a soft female voice.

"Yeeeeeaaaahhh!" With a blood-curdling shriek, a team of small, vicious creatures pounced on him. Prince Phillip fought fiercely, but he was outnumbered. Suddenly Maleficent materialized before him. "I set my trap for a peasant and I catch a prince!" said Maleficent. "Away with him!"

Howling with laughter, the ghoul-ish creatures pushed the helpless prince out the door.

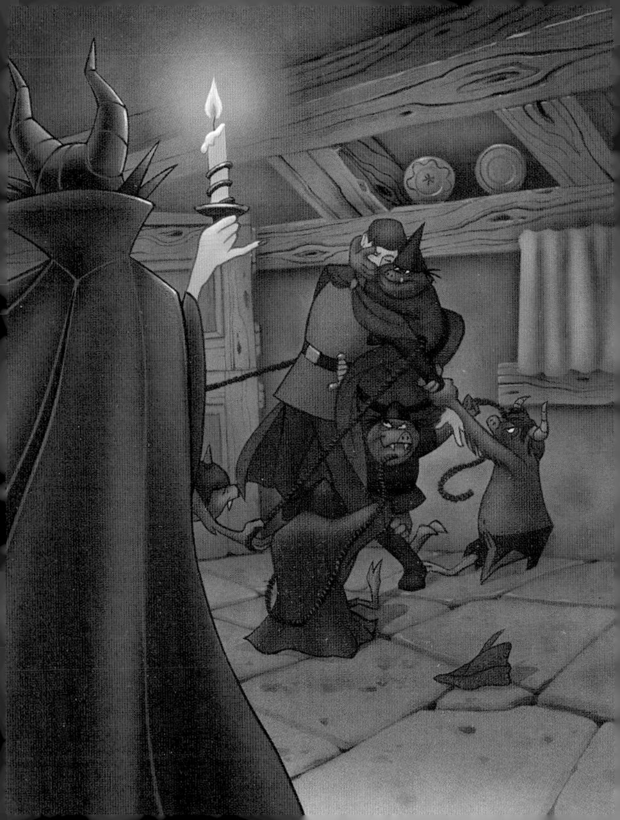

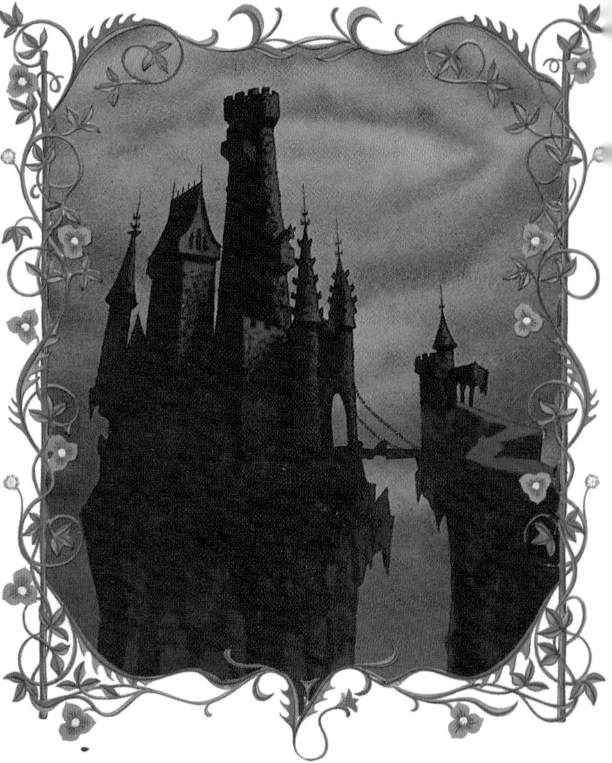

CHAPTER NINE

By the time the fairies got to the cottage, all that was left of Prince Phillip was his cap.

"Maleficent has the prince!" cried Merryweather.

"At the Forbidden Mountains!" Flora added.

"We must go there!" cried Flora.

Without another word, the fairies were off. Soon they came upon the jagged spires of Maleficent's decaying castle. Once inside, they could hear loud screeches coming from one wing of the castle. They flew toward the noise at once and saw a crackling bonfire in the room below. As Maleficent watched from her throne, her creatures danced wildly around the fire, screaming and screeching.

"What a pity Prince Phillip can't be here to enjoy the celebration," she said. "Come. We must go to the dungeon and cheer him up."

The fairies fluttered silently behind, following her down a steep,

drafty stairwell to a heavy wooden
door. Inside Prince Phillip was shack-
led to the wall with chains.

"Oh, come now, Prince Phillip,"
Maleficent tut-tutted. "Why so
melancholy? A wondrous future

lies before you. Observe . . ."

Her crystal ball began to glow with an image of Aurora. "There is your peasant!"

Prince Phillip gasped and pulled at his chains.

"Come, my pet," Maleficent said to her raven.

When Maleficent was gone, the fairies flew out from their hiding place. Waving their wands, they destroyed the prince's chains and the lock on the door. Prince Phillip was free.

"Wait!" Flora warned Prince Phillip. "Take this enchanted Shield of Virtue and this mighty Sword of Truth. These weapons of righteousness will triumph over evil!"

When they reached the top of the stairs, a loud squawk from

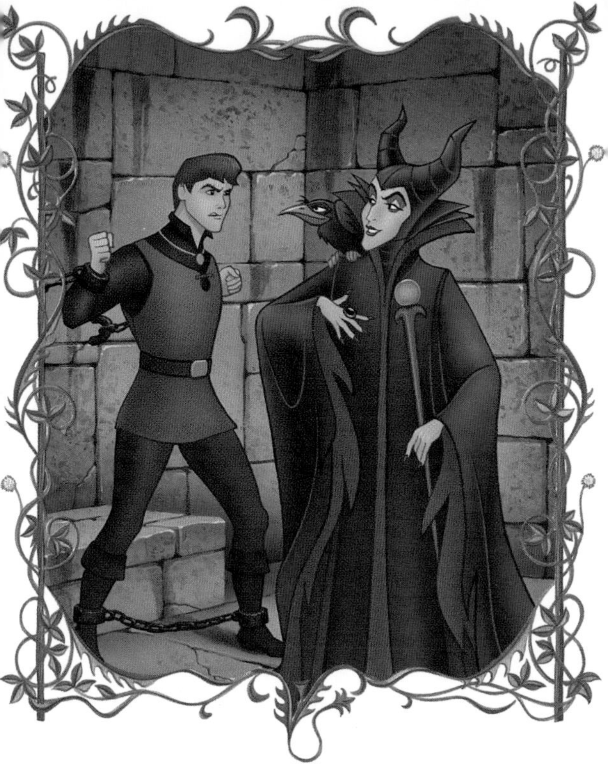

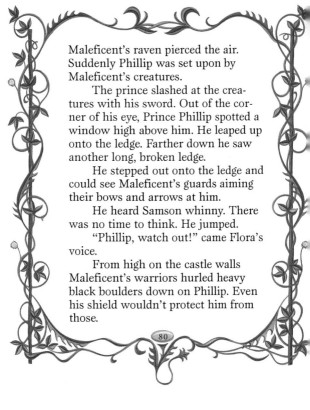

Maleficent's raven pierced the air. Suddenly Phillip was set upon by Maleficent's creatures.

The prince slashed at the creatures with his sword. Out of the corner of his eye, Prince Phillip spotted a window high above him. He leaped up onto the ledge. Farther down he saw another long, broken ledge.

He stepped out onto the ledge and could see Maleficent's guards aiming their bows and arrows at him.

He heard Samson whinny. There was no time to think. He jumped.

"Phillip, watch out!" came Flora's voice.

From high on the castle walls Maleficent's warriors hurled heavy black boulders down on Phillip. Even his shield wouldn't protect him from those.

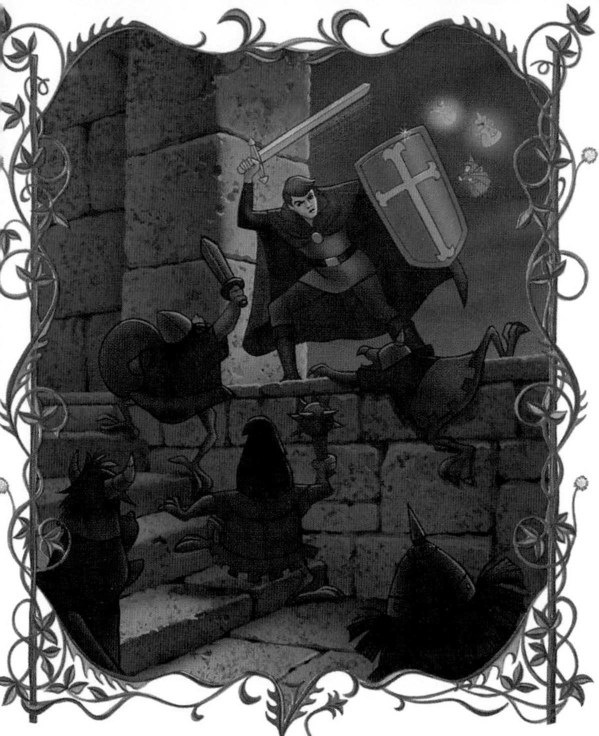

Flora waved her magic wand, and—
POOF—they instantly changed into
harmless bubbles.

Quickly Prince Phillip and Samson
sped across the courtyard. Then
Merryweather looked up and saw the
raven. Clutching her wand, she began to
chase him.

Merryweather shot fairy dust at the
bird but missed each time. Finally—
zzzing!—she got him! Instantly the raven
was turned to stone.

"No!" cried Maleficent. "My pet!"

Then she spotted Prince Phillip gal-
loping across the creaking drawbridge.
Samson leapt across to safety just as the
bridge started to rise. Maleficent's eyes
burned with fury.

Ahead of him was a crevice in the
earth just narrow enough to leap over,
and beyond that was King Stefan's castle.

CRRRRAACCCCK! Maleficent
hurled a lightning bolt that hit the
crevice, opening it too wide to cross.
Maleficent watched, her rage boiling
inside her as Samson slid down the
steep piles of rocks and struggled to
climb up the other side. Then she
raised her staff high.

"A forest of thorns shall be his
tomb!" she cried out. Then all at once
there was the CRRRRAACCCCK! of

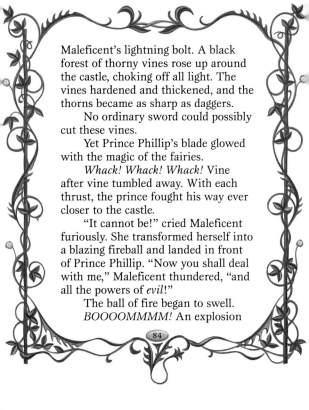

Maleficent's lightning bolt. A black forest of thorny vines rose up around the castle, choking off all light. The vines hardened and thickened, and the thorns became as sharp as daggers.

No ordinary sword could possibly cut these vines.

Yet Prince Phillip's blade glowed with the magic of the fairies.

Whack! Whack! Whack! Vine after vine tumbled away. With each thrust, the prince fought his way ever closer to the castle.

"It cannot be!" cried Maleficent furiously. She transformed herself into a blazing fireball and landed in front of Prince Phillip. "Now you shall deal with me," Maleficent thundered, "and all the powers of *evil*!"

The ball of fire began to swell. *BOOOOMMMM!* An explosion

shook the ground; the ball of fire
seemed to swallow everything
around it.

Then Maleficent transformed
herself into a huge dragon.

HHHHHAAAAAA! A fiery
blast from the dragon shot toward
the prince. When Phillip scrambled
behind a thicket of vines, he knew
that the dragon had lost sight of him.
He waited and watched as the shad-
ow of the dragon's head came closer
and closer.

Then the prince jumped out of hiding and struck the dragon with his sword.

Enraged, the dragon blew fire over the entire forest. Phillip was surrounded in flames!

"Up this way!" cried Flora.

Phillip's only path of escape was up a smooth cliff. Digging in with his fingers, he scrambled to the top.

The prince barely had time to get to his feet before the dragon materialized before him.

Prince Phillip was trapped! As the dragon lunged toward him and opened its mouth, Prince Phillip raised his magic shield.

HHHHHAAAAA! The flame hit the shield and it flew out of the prince's hands.

He held up his sword, but it was

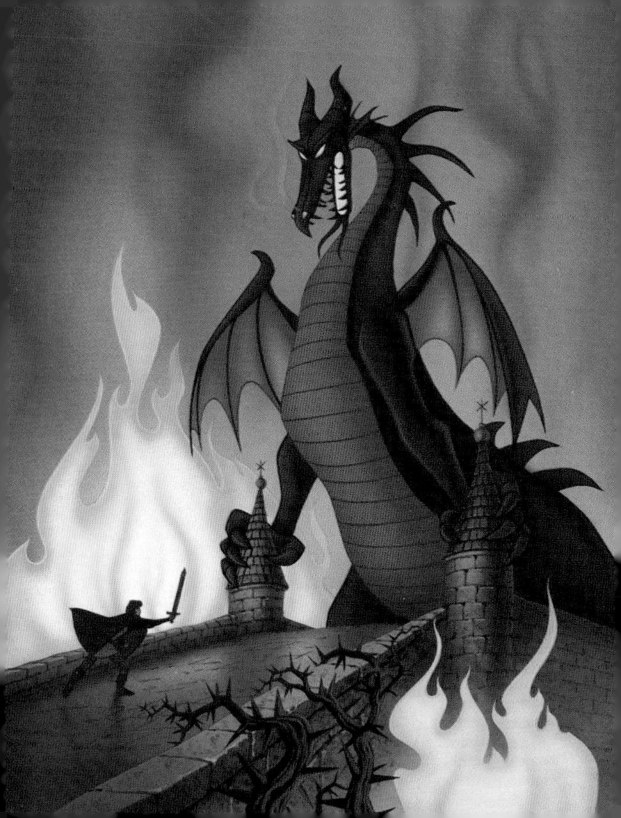

of little use against the dragon's
flames.

   Then the fairies sent a flurry of
magic dust toward his sword and
chanted, "Sword of Truth fly swift and
sure, that Evil die and Good endure!"

   Phillip drew back and threw the

sword, and it sliced through the air.

The anguished screech of the dragon left no doubt that the sword had
landed deep in its heart. With a bel-
low that seemed to blot out all other
sounds on earth, the dragon plunged
over the cliff to its fiery death.

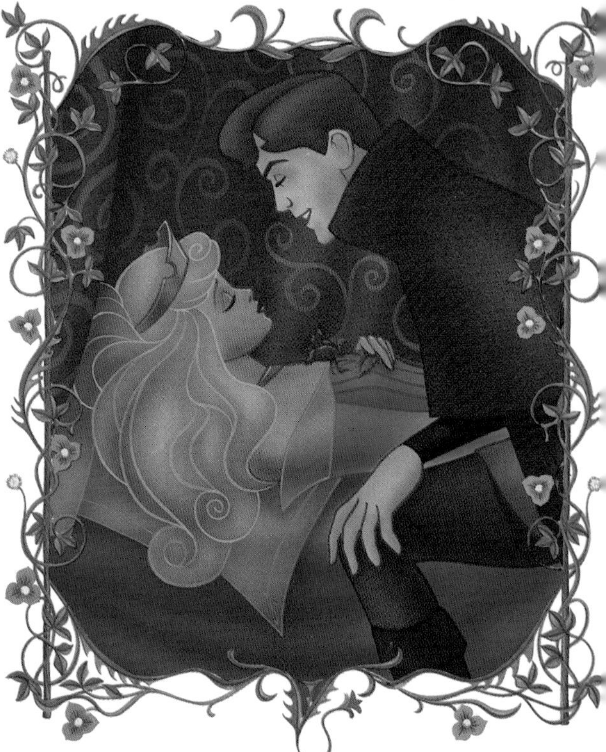

CHAPTER TEN

The prince sank to his knees, exhausted. Around him fluttered three white lights. He knew that the fairies had saved his life and ended Maleficent's evil. All around him the thorny vines were shrinking, and the fire died out, the smoke vanishing into the sky. In the distance King Stefan's castle glimmered as if washed by a spring rain.

Inside the castle, the courtiers and townspeople were still fast asleep. Prince Phillip, escorted by the fairies, went straight to the castle tower to the room in which Aurora lay sleeping.

The prince pushed the door open. Aurora was almost as lovely asleep as

she was awake. The prince knelt beside her and planted a soft kiss on her lips.

Slowly Aurora's eyes flickered once, then twice. When they caught sight of Prince Phillip, they opened fully. Then a warm smile brought the princess's face back to life. All over the castle, people slowly began to awaken.

In the throne room King Stefan picked up his head and turned to King Hubert. "You were saying?"

"Oh, yes!" King Hubert mumbled. "Well, my son Phillip says he's going to marry a—"

The blare of a trumpet fanfare cut him off. All eyes focused on the top of the grand stairway where Prince Phillip and Princess Aurora appeared. The young couple approached the

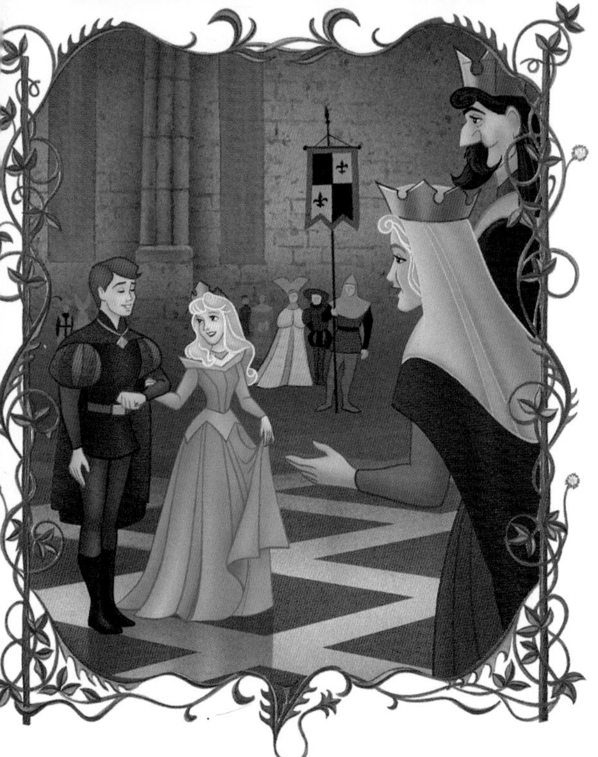

throne. When Aurora got close to
the queen, she received a most lov-
ing embrace.

"What does this mean, boy?"
King Hubert asked. Then, with a
sigh, he shrugged his shoulders
and swayed to the music.

From a balcony the three fairies
watched as the prince and the princess
danced.

"What's the matter, Fauna?" Flora
asked in a kindly tone.

Fauna sniffed. "Oh, I just love
happy endings."

"I do, too," Flora said, watching Aurora dance in her sky blue dress. *"Blue?"* she blurted.

Zzzing! She waved her wand and turned it pink.

Now Merryweather's smile disappeared. "Blue!" she demanded. *Zzzing!* went her wand.

On the dance floor, Aurora looked lovingly into the eyes of her prince. Her most magical dream had come true.